For K&E - A.L.
For Leonie - L.B.

PUFFIN BOOKS

UK | USA | Canada | Ireland | Australia
India | New Zealand | South Africa
Puffin Books is part of the Penguin Random House group of companies
whose addresses can be found at global.penguinrandomhouse.com.
www.penguin.co.uk   www.puffin.co.uk   www.ladybird.co.uk

Penguin
Random House
UK

First published 2019
001

Printed in China
A CIP catalogue record for this book is available from the British Library

ISBN: 978–0–141–38665–2
All correspondence to:
Puffin Books, Penguin Random House Children's,
80 Strand, London WC2R 0RL

Style it!

Thanks Kittie
xx

The Fairytale Hairdresser

and

THUMBELINA

Abie Longstaff
&
Lauren Beard

PUFFIN

Kittie Lacey was the best hairdresser in all the land.

Today, there was an extra-long queue outside her salon. It was nearly time for the Flower Festival, and everyone wanted a special floral hairstyle.

Sleeping Beauty and Prince Florian
wanted roses in their hair.

Rapunzel asked for a long plait of ivy.

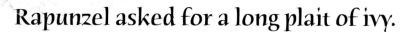

And Mr Gingerbread Man chose
a giant foxglove to wear at the festival.

Suddenly there was a flutter at the salon window, and in flew Bluebird with Thumbelina on his back. This tiny girl was the last of the Flower People. All the others had mysteriously disappeared from Fairyland.

"It makes me sad to think that I'm the only one left," said Thumbelina. "Let's look at your baby book," Kittie suggested. "That always cheers you up."

MY BABY BOOK

I was born: in a flower
At birth I weighed:
the same as a matchstick
My first bed was:
an acorn
My first bath was:
in a teaspoon

My best friend is:
Bluebird. He flies me
everywhere.
My family is: me,
my mummy and my daddy.
I'm adopted, and they wanted
me so very much.
Mummy and Daddy chose
my name because: I'm no
bigger than a thumb.

Bluebird

BFF

Fun fact about me:
I don't have wings like the other Flower People.

"The Flower Festival is my favourite time of year," said Thumbelina. "I love dancing among the wildflowers – although I wish there were other Flower People to dance with . . ."

Kittie gave her a hug. "You won't be alone," she said. "We'll all be there with you."

"Thanks, Kittie," said Thumbelina. She showed Kittie all the outfits she'd made for the Flower Festival. "I'm going to Goblin Market tomorrow to sell them," she said. "Good luck!" said Kittie.

The next day, Kittie was putting sweetpea flowers in the Sugar Plum Fairy's hair when Bluebird arrived in a panic.

"What's wrong?" asked Kittie. "Has something happened to Thumbelina?"
Bluebird nodded and tugged Kittie's hair.

"You want me to come with you?" said Kittie. "I can't fly on you – I'm too big."
"I can help with that," said the Sugar Plum Fairy. She waved her wand
and Kittie shrank

down . . .

down . . .

down . . .

. . . until she was small enough to climb onto Bluebird's back.

"Let's go!" she cried.

Bluebird flew high over Fairyland, past the meadow of wildflowers, above the woods and all the way to the mountains.
"There's Goblin Market!" Kittie called, and Bluebird zoomed down.

I ONLY HAVE **PIES** FOR YOU

Today's Special...
PUMPKIN PIE

APPLEY EVER AFTER

HIDDEN GEMS

Bluebird landed right in the middle of the market, and Kittie rushed through the crowds to Thumbelina's stall.

"Thumbelina?" Kittie called. But there was no answer.

"I just saw Thumbelina," said Mrs Field Mouse. "She was walking away from the market with the Goblin King. She went that way!"

"Thank you," said Kittie. She ran through the market . . .

. . . and stumbled across the entrance to a deep, dark tunnel.
"The Goblin King must be in here!" gasped Kittie.

Kittie bravely stepped into the tunnel.
It was very dark and very narrow. She felt her way
along the walls until she came to an opening.

Kittie peered through.
She took one, two, three steps into . . .

The Goblin King's Throne Room! The walls were covered in cages, and Kittie could see tiny grey people inside. At the end of the room was a huge throne and on it sat the Goblin King himself, clapping his hands in glee.

"My collection is complete!" he cried. "Now I have ALL the Flower People."
He opened a bag and pulled out a little person. Kittie stifled a gasp . . .

It was Thumbelina!

"Ah, you are so little and colourful," he said. "I'll put you in this cage here, with the Prince of Flowers." The Goblin King locked the cage – Thumbelina was trapped!

The king scuttled off, cackling to himself, and when his footsteps had faded Kittie crept to Thumbelina's cage.

"Kittie!" cried Thumbelina. "Help!"
"Please hurry," said Rowan, the Prince of Flowers.
"We're wilting away!"
"Don't worry, love," said Kittie. "I'm going to set
you all free."

Kittie took a hairpin out of her toolbelt and twisted it into the lock.

One by one, she opened every cage.

"Quick! Let's go!" she whispered.

But just then came the thud of footsteps . . .

Thud
Thud
Thud

The Goblin King was coming back!

"Aha!" cried the Goblin King. He grinned greedily at Kittie.
"Another small person for my collection. Excellent!"

Kittie thought for a moment. She had a very clever idea . . .
"I'm not small enough," she said. "I can't fit into this cage."

"Yes, you can!" said the king. "Even I can fit in there!"
"I bet you can't," said Kittie.

"I can!" said the king. "I'll prove it!"

The Goblin King squeezed himself
into one of the empty cages.
Quick as a flash, Kittie closed the
cage door and pulled a ribbon from
her belt. "This should hold you till
the Fairyland guards get here,"
she said, tying the ribbon as tightly
as she could.

"Hurry, everyone!" she shouted,
and they sped down the tunnel and
out into the sunshine, where
Bluebird was waiting for them.

"Thank you for saving us," said Rowan. He bowed to Kittie.
"You are very welcome," replied Kittie.
Thumbelina took his hand. "Come and celebrate with us at the Flower Festival," she said.

"But we're all grey from the darkness," said the prince. "It will take months for the sun to bring our colours back."
"I can help with that," said Kittie. "Let's fly back to the salon!"

Kittie and Thumbelina gave everyone a beautiful make-over.

"Come on, everyone," said Kittie. "It's time for the Flower Festival!"

Everyone was amazed to see the Flower People in Fairyland again!
They clapped and cheered in jubilation.

Thumbelina had never been so happy. Her heart spilled over with joy, and all at once – *whoosh!* – two beautiful wings blossomed behind her. She laughed in delight and took Rowan's arm, and they danced for hours.

Prince Rowan gave Kittie a special crown of daisies. "Now everyone will know of your bravery and kindness to the Flower People," he said.

"Hooray for Kittie!" cried Thumbelina, and everyone cheered.